Paddington
Weighs In

CARNIVAL

One day, Paddington was making his way home to number thirty-two Windsor Gardens with the morning shopping, when he came across a most unusual sign.

It was hanging on a machine outside the entrance to a large building, and it said:

TEST YOUR WEIGHT – FREE!

Paddington liked anything free and he lost no time in trying out the offer.

But as he gazed at the dial he nearly fell over backwards with surprise, for the needle had gone right off the end of the scale.

It was a long time since Paddington had last weighed himself, but even allowing for all the buns and marmalade sandwiches he had eaten in between, it still came as a shock.

Looking most upset, he was about to go on his way again when he caught sight of yet another notice fixed to the door of the building.

This one said, quite simply: YOU HAVE A WEIGHT PROBLEM? THEN DON'T DELAY — COME IN TODAY.

Paddington needed no second bidding. Pulling his shopping basket behind him, he hurried into the building as fast as his legs would carry him and made his way towards an imposing looking counter marked RECEPTION.

"Excuse me," he announced, raising his hat politely. "I've come about my weight. I think I may have a problem."

The receptionist eyed Paddington doubtfully. "I'm not sure if we are taking on any bears at present," he said. "Er . . . how many pounds did you have in mind?"

Paddington opened his suitcase and, after carefully making sure the man couldn't see what he was doing, peered inside the secret compartment.

"I think I could manage five," he said. "Especially if I go without buns for a while."

The receptionist looked most impressed.
"*Five* pounds!" he exclaimed. "My word! You're just the sort of client we at WEIGHT-SHREDDERS like to have."

He pointed towards a nearby door. "Please come this way. I'll fetch our Mr. Constantine."

"You might like to start off with one of his pummels before he shows you the ropes," he continued. "Mr. Constantine likes to get cracking straight away, and they work wonders."

Paddington licked his lips. Losing weight by eating sounded very good value indeed.

"I think I'll have two pummels, if I may," he said hopefully.

"Two?" repeated the man in awe. "I don't think anyone's ever had *two* of Mr. Constantine's pummels before. Are you sure?"

"Quite sure," said Paddington firmly. It was a long time since his elevenses.

As the door swung shut Paddington gazed around. It was quite unlike any dining-room he'd ever been in before. Even the table looked more like a bed.

So much so that when he climbed on top in order to test it, he suddenly felt very sleepy indeed.

Paddington wasn't sure how long he slept, but it seemed as though he'd just closed his eyes when what felt like a ton weight suddenly landed on top of him.

He tried to sit up, but nothing moved, and as he opened his eyes he saw to his alarm that a large, bearded figure had him pinned to the table.

Mr. Constantine gave a broad beam and, before Paddington had a chance to say anything, he began pounding away with his fists again.

"Is good, no?" he chuckled.

"No, it isn't!" yelled Paddington, as he tried to escape.

The receptionist had said Mr. Constantine liked to get cracking, but never in his wildest dreams had he pictured it being quite so painful.

Mr. Constantine looked puzzled. "You do not like my pummels?" he enquired. "I thought you were going to have two lots. I try again . . ."

"No, thank you!" cried Paddington. "I'd sooner you showed me the ropes instead, if you don't mind."

"The ropes?" Mr. Constantine frowned again, and then his face cleared. "Ah! . . . I understand. I lift you up . . . so . . ."

"Hooray! Good for tummy . . . no?"

"No!" shouted Paddington, as he clung on for dear life.

"In that case . . ." Mr. Constantine lifted Paddington down and placed him on one of the machines, "we will try the vibrator massage."

"I push the button . . . so, and Hey Presto!"

"Ooooh!" cried Paddington, as he felt his whole body begin to shake. "He . . . he . . . helllp!"

"You want faster?" shouted Mr. Constantine excitedly.

"N . . . n . . . nooo . . . I . . d . . . d . doooon't!" shrieked Paddington.

"Good! Good!" bellowed Mr. Constantine, unable to hear Paddington's voice over the noise from the machine. "After this we try the hot steam bath, and then the ice-cold shower."

B ut Paddington had had more than
enough. Somehow or other he managed to
wriggle free, and before Mr. Constantine
could stop him he staggered across the room,
through the door . . . and out into the hall
. . . landing in a heap by the reception desk.

"I'm afraid you can't lie there," said the
receptionist severely. "Someone might trip
over you."

"Perhaps," he said brightly, "you might like to have your lunch now? It's almost one o'clock."

Paddington sat up. "Oh, yes, please," he gasped. "I'd like that *very* much."

"Be careful you don't spill any," warned the man. "We don't allow seconds."

"*Seconds*!" Paddington stared at the spoon as if he could hardly believe his eyes. "I haven't even had my *firsts* yet!"

"Think yourself lucky you're getting carrot juice," said the man sternly. "Some of our patients only get hot water on their first day."

"Carrot juice!" exclaimed Paddington bitterly. "Five pounds for a spoonful of carrot juice!" He gave the receptionist one of his hardest ever stares.

"Oh, dear," said the receptionist, wilting under Paddington's gaze. "I think there must be some mistake. I didn't mean five pounds in money, I meant five pounds in *weight*. After all, this *is* a health clinic, you know, not a restaurant."

"It doesn't sound very healthy to me," said Paddington. "It doesn't sound very healthy at all. I'm glad I haven't paid."

A nd before the man had time to say any more he disappeared out of the building even faster than he'd entered it. In fact, he went so fast he collided with the weighing machine, and for a moment or two, stood clutching it as if his very life was at stake.

And then, as he gradually got his breath back, he made a very surprising discovery. His weight had gone down again. In fact, it was almost back to normal.

Paddington was just deciding that perhaps Mr. Constantine's pummels worked wonders after all, when he made a second discovery.

As he picked up his shopping basket the needle went right off the scale again.

"Oh, dear!" he exclaimed, as the truth dawned on him.

His groceries were at least double his own weight and the two together were more than the machine could take.

"I think," he announced to the world in general, "there should be scales in every street. People might not spend so much on their shopping then. Or on health clinics!"

This story comes from
PADDINGTON'S BLUE PETER STORYBOOK
and is based on the television film.
It has been specially written by
Michael Bond for younger children.

Carnival
An imprint of the Children's Division
of the Collins Publishing Group
8 Grafton Street, London W1X 3LA

Published by Carnival 1989

ISBN 0 00 194535 1

Printed & bound in Great Britain by
PURNELL BOOK PRODUCTION LIMITED
A MEMBER OF BPCC plc